T4

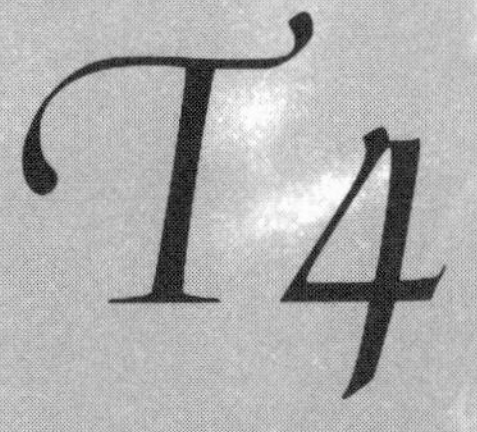

A Novel in Verse

by Ann Clare LeZotte

Houghton Mifflin Company
Boston 2008

This book is dedicated to the loving memory
of my parents,

Bess George LeZotte
and
Edward Harrison LeZotte

www.houghtonmifflinbooks.com

The text of this book is set in Calisto MT.

Library of Congress Cataloging-in-Publication Data

LeZotte, Ann Clare.
T4 : a novel in verse / written by Ann Clare LeZotte.
p. cm.

Summary: When the Nazi party takes control of Germany, thirteen-year-old Paula, who is deaf, finds her world-as-she-knows-it turned upside down, as she is taken into hiding to protect her from the new law nicknamed T4.

ISBN-13: 978-0-547-04684-6

[1. Novels in verse. 2. Deaf—Fiction. 3. People with disabilities—Fiction. 4. Aktion T4 (Germany)—Fiction. 5. Germany—History—1933–1945—Fiction.] I. Title. II. Title: Tee four.

PZ7.5.L49Taal 2008
[Fic]—dc22

2007047737

Printed in the United States of America
MP 10 9 8 7 6 5 4 3 2 1

The best and most beautiful things in the
world cannot be seen or even touched—
they must be felt with the heart.

—Helen Keller

Hear the Voice of the Poet

Hear the voice of the poet!
I see the past, future, and present.
I am Deaf, but I have heard
The beauty of song

And I wish to share it with
Young readers.
A poem can be simple,
About a cat or a red
Wheelbarrow.

Or it can illuminate the lives
Of people who lived, loved,
And died. You can make
People think or feel

For other people, if you
Write poetry. In *T4,* the facts
About history are true, and
My characters tell the story.

I was born

In a little house
On a street
With tall poplar trees.

I could see
Bluish hills
In the distance.

That was my home.
But my country,
Germany,
Was not my home.

Our leader,
Adolf Hitler,
And the Nazi Party
Hated
People like me.

When my mother was pregnant

With me, she was exposed
To rubella, or German measles,

A common cause of hearing loss
In infancy. I wasn't completely deaf

Until I had a high fever at sixteen
Months old. I don't remember what

I heard before then. My mother said
I clapped my hands when she spoke.

I loved bird song and our cuckoo clock.

In the beginning

My small dog, Schatze, barked at my back.
Later she learned to tap me on the leg
When she wanted to be petted. She danced
On her back legs so I would give her a bone.

My parents and grandparents and my sister,
Clara, loved me even though I was Disabled.
Father painted roses on the wooden bed
I shared with Clara. Mother baked fresh bread

And let me have a piece while it was still warm.
Grandfather played the fiddle. I held on to the
Instrument so I could feel the fast folk music.
Grandmother pointed at the night sky. I saw
Bright Casseopeia, Orion, and a shooting star.

Fair and dark

I was fair like Father;
Clara was dark like Mother.

Father and I
Loved being in the sun;
Mother and Clara
Sat in front of the hearth's fire.

We were robust like horses.
They were elegant and slinky like cats.

We enjoyed eating big meals.
They took small bites of a single radish.

We snored like buzz saws
Or a hornets' nest.
Their dreams were silent
And beautiful like flowers.

I didn't learn to speak

The way most children do.
I put my fingers on the vocal cords
Of my family.
I wanted to feel
What talking sounded like.

I tried to open my mouth
And make sounds,
But nobody understood me.
They said I should keep quiet.

I watched the lips
Of my relatives
When they told stories.
I could see words
Being formed on their mouths.
It's called lip-reading.

I saw books and letters.
I knew people were expressing
Ideas with language.
But when I was very young,

I couldn't communicate.
I was trapped in my silence,
As if under a veil.

This made me feel upset
And angry sometimes.
I put my face in my pillow
And sobbed and sighed.

What I Saw

My visual

Sense

Was so

Strong.

If

A breeze

Shook

The leaves

On

A tree

I

Would

Shriek

With

Delight.

If

People

Ran fast

Past me

It looked

Like

A tidal

Wave.

Even

The motion

Of

A hand

Waving

Goodbye

Startled

Me.

Father Josef

The Catholic priest in my town
Decided to teach me my name.

He drew the letters
P-A-U-L-A B-E-C-K-E-R
On a sheet of paper.
He pointed to the words
And then to me.

I tried to trace the letters
With a piece of charcoal.
He held my hand
In the correct position.

I stared at my name,
Paula Becker,
Until I memorized it.

I made hand signs

For the objects I saw around me.
I put my fingertips against my lips
When I was hungry.

I rubbed my eyes
To show
I was tired.

I shook my head
And snorted
In imitation
Of a horse.

I bared my teeth and crept
Across the floor like a wolf.

A rock was made with my fist.
I waved my arms to say "the wind."

I put the palm of my hand
On top of my heart
And then pointed at my mother
And father and sister
And grandparents.
That meant I loved them.

I counted on my fingers,
And when the number
Was more than ten
I made markings on a stick.

Old Marthe

Lived on a farm
Outside town.
Some people said
She was a witch.

She always wore
A long brown coat
And galoshes,
Even when she slept.

She gave
Remedies
To the sick
And Disabled.

She made them from
Items she gathered
In the woods: flowers,
Bark, weeds, nuts.

She trapped small
Animals for food
And wore their bones
Around her neck or
Boiled them for soup.

In my sixth year
My mother took me
To her place.

I was scared
But fascinated
By her
Ramshackle house.

Marthe melted a candle
In a pot
And poured hot wax
Into my ears.

It hurt a lot.
She made me sit
On a stool
As it cooled.

Then she took
A paring knife
And carefully
Removed the hard wax.

Marthe cupped her palms
Over my ears,
Said a prayer, and quickly
Removed her hands.

She was yelling
And stomping her feet
Like she was dancing.
Her black cat,
Mittennacht,
Ran out the door.

Mother and I were
Hoping she could
Make me hear,
But she couldn't.

On the way home
My mother cried.
And I still wanted
To be a regular girl
Rather than a dumb animal.

In 1939

I was thirteen years old.
My family and our neighbors
Had learned to accept me.
I was the deaf girl with pigtails
In a red and yellow calico dress.

Father Josef taught me
To write the whole alphabet.
I could read a couple of books.
I carried a pad and pencil

To write down answers
To questions I was asked
Or to ask for a pound of
Sugar or butter at the store.

Many people in town had
Learned my word signs.
It was still difficult
For me to speak.

I moved my lips
When I prayed in church.

I could feel the organ
Playing through the floor.
It shook
My whole body and soul.

At home I helped
My mother cook, clean,
And look after
Clara and Schatze.

It would seem
That my life was good.
But something terrible
Was about to happen.

Action T4

Was the Nazi program that
Almost cost me my life.

It was named after
The address of its
Headquarters in Berlin,

Tiergartenstrasse 4.

T4 was run by doctors

Not soldiers
Or the Gestapo,
The secret police.

The directors were
Dr. Philip Bouhler
And Karl Brandt,
Hitler's private physician.

They were not good doctors
Who wanted to help people.
They were under direct orders
To kill the mentally ill
And people with disabilities.

It made no difference to them
If we were children or adults.
It was just a job to them.

Eugenics

The Nazis believed that certain people
Were superior to other people.

They wanted the human race
To become an "Aryan" race.
They wanted to get rid of people
Who they thought
Polluted the gene pool.
This is called eugenics,
Or "racial hygiene."

They wanted perfect people
To give birth to more perfect people.
They imagined Germany as a master race
Who would rule the world.

They attacked Jews, people of color,
Homosexuals, and Gypsies, among others.

And they decided
Disabled people
Were "useless eaters"
Who were "unfit to live."

Patients in institutions

Were the first to die.

The Nazis knew that many Germans
Would be opposed to Action T4
If they knew the whole truth.
So they had to hide the facts.

They said "specialist children's wards,"
But they meant children-killing centers.
They said "final medical assistance,"
But they meant murder.

Euthanasia

Is the act or practice
Of killing or permitting the death of
    hopelessly sick
Or injured people or animals with as little
    pain as
Possible for mercy reasons.

It is a controversial procedure and sad
For everyone. A decision is usually made
By a patient or her loved ones.

The Nazis claimed the Disabled
Were so miserable in their lives
That they didn't care if they lived or died.
They pretended they were helping us.

But I wanted
My life.
I liked being a part
Of the larger
Everything.

My parents were aware

These things
Were happening
In our country.

But they didn't tell me.

I used to play
Outside all day.
I'd jump rope, climb
Trees, and pick the tart
Little apples to eat.

I'd lie on the grass
And study my picture
Bible or the newspaper.

But now they wanted me
To stay in the house.

The seasons were changing.
Our roof sprang a leak
And the rain fell
Into buckets and the bathtub.

Schatze and I were bored.

But the adults were
Always
Looking out the window
And waiting for a knock
On the door.

A Knock on the Door

One night
In March 1940,
Father Josef
Came to our house.

It was snowing and raining,
Making the roads icy.

Mother sat him by the fire
And gave him a glass of hot cider.
He smoked a long pipe.

After he warmed up
His thin face was still pale
And his hands were shaking.

He told my parents
To put me back in bed with Clara
Before he spoke with them.

I went to my room as I was told.
But many years later
My mother told me what he said.

That was the night
Terror came into our home.
Although I was so young,
I knew that moment
Was a dividing line
Between my childhood
And whatever came next.

The Story of Anny Wodl

Father Josef had visited Austria.
He met a woman named Anny Wodl.
She told him this story.

"I bore a Disabled child in 1934.
He had trouble walking and talking.
The doctors could not tell me the cause
Of his disability.
I didn't know if he was suffering.
I put him in an institution
When he was four years old.

I became aware of the policies against
Disabled people.
I was afraid for my son's life.

The Austrian authorities
Would not help me,
So I appealed to Berlin.

A man named Dr. Jekelius
Contacted me.

He made it clear
That he agreed
With the Nazis' policies.

I realized then
That my son
Was going to die.

I begged Dr. Jekelius
To make his death
Quick and painless.
He promised me.

But later
When I saw his corpse
He had a pained look on his face.

Most people I knew
Disapproved
Of these actions
But they were
Too afraid to say so."

Father said

He'd never heard
Such a terrible thing
In his life.
He made a vow
To protect me
At the expense
Of his own life.

Father Josef said my father was noble

But that he couldn't protect me in my home.
In time,
The Nazis would look for me and find me
there.

Father Josef told my parents
That he would take me with him and hide me
In a safe place
Until the end of the war.

My family was heartbroken,
But they agreed to let me go.

I packed

A few

Of my

Favorite things

In a shawl

Grandmother knitted:

A teddy bear named Emma,

A spool of brown thread and a needle,

An old fairy tale book with the story

Of Hansel and Gretel,

And my pocket-size pad and pencil.

We all exchanged hugs and kisses.

It was the hardest thing

I ever had to do,

But I tried not to look back.

I fell asleep next to Father Josef. He had a
Blanket over his lap. He tucked it around me
As he drove his car out of our secluded town.
The movement of the wheels under my seat
Soothed me like a lullaby.

I awoke in a barn

Covered with straw
And a woolen blanket.

The moon
Was still visible in the sky.

I felt a pit in my stomach.
I was hungry.

I cried when I remembered
I had left my family behind.

Soon, a lady appeared in the doorway

She waved for me to follow her into the big
house.
I sat at the kitchen table and
She gave me bread and milk.

She made certain movements with her fingers
And took my hand to do the same thing.
She was trying to teach me
The official sign language alphabet of the
Deaf.
I learned to make the letters on one hand;
It's called finger-spelling.

She also taught me word signs for the objects
I saw in the house and garden:
Chair, bed, book, tree, grass, rabbit.

Language is a key.
I felt so many doors were opening to me.

The lady in the doorway was Stephanie
Holderlin.

Stephanie Holderlin

Was a retired schoolteacher.
She lived alone on a farm.
She knew Father Josef
And agreed to hide me.

She didn't agree with T4.
She kept books in her attic
That had been banned
And burned by the Nazis.

She had a Deaf pupil once.
She learned to use
German Sign Language
So she could teach him.

Not only did she teach me
To sign,
But I learned
To be brave
From her.

I put on Stephanie's lipstick

Staring into the oval mirror
On her vanity table.

It was a dark shade of red,
Sort of like the wing
Of a cardinal,
Or a fancy automobile.

I undid my hair.
It had a natural wave.

I noticed
I was getting
Little yellow hairs
In my armpits
And on my privates.

Another Knock on the Door

It was three in the morning and
The Gestapo was at the door!

By that time I had stopped
Sleeping in the barn.
I was curled up
On a pile of feather beds
In Stephanie's spare bedroom.

She sent me running
Out the back door to the barn.
She told me to sit in the dirty pigsty
In my white nightgown
And to be still, keep quiet.

I shivered from the cold
And the smell and fear.
After an hour of waiting,
Stephanie came to get me.

She was talking fast;
I read her lips.

"The monsters asked me
If I have a Jewish child
Living in my home.
One of our neighbors
Must have seen you,
Although you rarely go
Out of the house,
And reported us.

Why don't they mind
Their own business?"

She'd told them a former student
Had stopped by briefly.
The secret police listened to her
And left. But it wasn't safe
For me to be there anymore.

Two days later

Father Josef came to pick me up.
I was happy to see him,
But I was sad to be leaving Stephanie.
I hoped I'd see her again someday.

Father Josef
Told me
He had visited
My family.

He said
Mother had been ill
But she was feeling better.
Father was working hard
But he missed me.

Schatze
Still looked for me
In the woods.
Father Josef
Reached into his pocket
And pulled out

A watercolor
Painting of two flowers.
And underneath them
Clara had written
Both of our names.

We drove two hours

To a church with a homeless shelter.

A Lutheran priest,
Father Michael,
Looked after me
During the months
I spent there.

He was nearly bald
And his face was rosy.

He had been concerned
About the welfare
Of the sick and Disabled
Even before the war.

Like a growing number
Of clergymen,
He wasn't afraid to speak
Out against T4.

At the shelter,
I watched the people around me.

They were talking about the crimes
That were being committed.

I learned things I couldn't believe were true.

They said

Disabled children
Were being taken
Out of their homes
Against
Their parents' wishes.

They were put
In hospitals and
Nursing homes.

They said a majority of two
Among three or four
Attending physicians
Was enough to issue
A death warrant.

They said
The children were transferred
To six killing stations,
The village of Grafeneck

In the Black Forest,
The “old jail”
At Brandenberg,
Berberg, Hartheim,
Sonnenstein,
And Hadamar.

Nobody said
Why
The doctors
Agreed
To do it.

Because nobody knew.

Dr. Bouhler

Insisted the deaths
Should be
Painless.

He didn't want
The patients
To know what was
Going to happen.

But they died of
Lethal injection
And starvation.

I was the only young girl at the shelter

So I spent a lot of time by myself.
I worked for my supper,
Serving soup and cleaning up
The tables and dishes.

One man watched me
As I swept the large room
And made up the cots.

He didn't frighten me.
I found him strange
And a little charming.

Because his clothes
Were rags pieced together
And he sometimes smelled
Like a wet animal,
They called him Poor Kurt.

Poor Kurt

Wrapped his dreams
Around him
Like a patchwork quilt.

He slept
Almost every night
At the shelter.
He slept all day too.

His bushy beard
Appeared to be gray,
But he never washed,
So I couldn't tell.

He said birds
Sat on his shoulders
In the park

And nibbled
Bits of bread
Caught in his beard.

Once I saw
A fox walk
Straight through
The door.
It drank milk from
Poor Kurt's mug.

He always
Rubbed his nose
As if he smelled
Something bad.

I pointed to his nose
To ask what it was.

He made the shape of
A building in the air
And pointed to the top,
The chimneys.

That was how
The Nazis got rid of
The bodies:
They burned them
In fiery ovens.

The death certificates were fake

Father Michael told us
A woman whose sister
Had been taken away
Showed him the paper.

It said
The cause of death
Was pneumonia.
They wouldn't let
Her see the body.

She received an urn
Filled with ashes.

She didn't even know
If they belonged to
Her sister,
Who was epileptic.

I was at the shelter for five months

When Poor Kurt
Shook me awake
And said, "Let's go
To Berlin."

"Why?" I asked,
Shaking my head
With outstretched arms.

Poor Kurt did
A pantomime
To let me know
His feet were itchy
And he wanted
A change of scenery.

He took a bowl
I was drying
From my hands

And seemed
To show me
I could help people
In the big city.

The Fathers
Had inspired
A feeling
Of charity
In me.

But did I dare
To walk into
The lions' den?

Berlin was the main
Place for the Nazis to be.

Father Josef hadn't come
To see me in a while.
I wondered if he had
Forgotten me.

I decided to go
Rather than stay hidden.

I wanted to see more
Of what was going on
In my country.

We decided to walk

All the way
To the city.
Poor Kurt said he knew the way.

I wrapped
My chapped feet in old cloths
And put my boots over them.
I still had my grandmother's shawl
To wrap around my shoulders.

We were in the middle of a forest
That looked like it was made of glass.
I wondered where the butterflies went
When the world was frozen over.

My hands had turned red and sore
And sometimes I couldn't feel my nose.
My blue eyes were large and dark and
My blond hair was dirty.
I had shrunk to the size of a beanpole.

Poor Kurt had a whistle
He said kept the bears away.

But I was afraid
He was calling them to us.

A car driven by SS

Drove past us.
They didn't stop.

The SS were an elite
Group of Nazi military.

They were scary—
Scarier than bears.

Germany's churches continued

To attack T4.

From a sermon
Of Clemens August von Galen,
Catholic bishop of Munster
In 1941:

"Woe to humanity,
Woe to the German people
If God's Holy
Commandment,

'Thou shall not kill,'
Is not only transgressed
But if the transgression
Is both tolerated
And carried out
Without
Punishment."

We saw a light in the woods

And stopped for the night.

Poor Kurt knocked on the door
Once, twice, three times.
He put his ear to the door
And then looked at me and shook
His head, meaning he heard nothing.
The light went out
Inside the small cabin.
Who lived there?

An owl flew past me,
Or a bat.
I shook my hands
In front of my face.

I looked up.
Orion's belt was visible above us all.
I made a wish on the evening star.

We were too tired not to stop,
So we waited and Kurt called out: "Help!"

Finally, a woman with sad, dark eyes
And a worried expression
Cracked open the door.

She looked at Poor Kurt
Suspiciously.
But when she caught
Sight of me,
I smiled as wide as I could.
She reached out a wrinkled hand
And gently pulled me in.
Poor Kurt too.

Seven people

In a room not big enough for three.
Two old people, the woman with the dark
eyes,
A man who looked like he could be her
brother,
A ten-year-old boy, a six-year-old girl, and a
baby.
They lay on top of each other to keep warm.
They lit a candle stub and prayed at sundown.
They ate bread that had turned black.
They put snow in a jug to make water.

Why did they live this way? They were Jews.

I shared my shawl and cloths

With the other children. I liked
Six-year-old Nelly. She
Reminded me of Clara.
We huddled together,
All nine of us,
And watched the door.
I darned my stocking
With the needle and thread
I brought along.
Nobody spoke.
We told stories
With our eyes
As we stared into
One another's faces.

I realized
I wasn't the only one
Who was hated.

Time passed

As slowly

As

An icicle

Melting

When

The sun

Shines.

I couldn't stay in that place

Any longer.
I told Poor Kurt, "We're going back
To the shelter."

I wanted our new friends
The Lindenbaums
To come along.

They were scared
To walk
Openly
Down the road.

I hoped Nelly
Would come with me, at least.
But the family didn't want to
Be separated.

I had just turned fourteen.
But I had a plan.
I would get Father Michael
To go back for them
In his car.

It was foolish
To head for the big city
If we could do good nearby.

I walked up a hill

In the evening.

I could see only
Four feet ahead of me.

I turned a corner
In an icy hedgerow
And there he was—
A moose.

He was very tall
And strong.

I looked up
At his antlers
And dark muzzle.

His eyes
Were clear,
Like stars.

He could
Have killed me.
But he didn't.

I stayed calm
And he walked
Around me.

I felt safe with him,
As in my father's arms.

Poor Kurt's knees

Kept knocking
And his teeth
Chattered
For hours
After.

I tried not to laugh,
But I felt light and happy.

We should have left bread crumbs
To find our way back. I think we
Walked in the same circle twice
Before we found the shelter.

I was scolded

For leaving the shelter,
But I could tell
Father Michael
Was relieved
To see me.

Father Josef
Was there too.
He gave me a big hug.

I was so excited.
They didn't understand
When I said they must go back
To save the Lindenbaums.

Poor Kurt
Related the story
As best he could.

Father Josef and Father Michael

Sat on a bench at the other side of the shelter.
I could see their lips moving.

They came back over to me and Poor Kurt.
Father Michael was wringing his hands.

Father Josef put his hand on my shoulder.
Poor Kurt listened to them with a frown.

When they moved away, he told me
With the signs I taught him that they would

Not be going back. I was shocked!
They thought we would all be in danger

Hiding Jews in our midst. I said, "But they are
Keeping me secret. What will happen to Nelly

And the baby, Paul?" Poor Kurt held on to me
And we both sobbed. Would anybody take

Pity on them? Not even God?

1941

Germany
Was caught up
In the Russian Campaign.

Hitler
Wanted to avoid
Public unrest at home.

He gave the order
To end T4.

But the killings didn't stop

I learned much later that individual physicians
Were making the choices themselves as to
    whether
Or not their patients were
"Fit for life."

As German cities were being bombed,
Inmates in institutions were being moved.
Many of them wound up dead.
Disabled adults were killed in gas chambers.

For decades after, they tried to hide
    the numbers.
It is estimated that 275,000 Disable people
Were "euthanized" by the Nazis.
Another 400,000 were sterilized
So they couldn't
Bear children like themselves.

When the American GIs

Occupied Germany
And World War II
Was finally over,

A handful of doctors
Who had worked
For Action T4
Were brought to justice.

Not Dr. Bouhler;
He committed suicide.
But Dr. Brandt was tried
And executed in a place
Called Nuremberg.

Some of the others continued
To practice medicine.

T4 became something people
Weren't willing to talk about
And remember.

But now I could go home

To my little house
On a street
With tall poplar trees

And bluish hills
In the distance.

Though
The war
Still
Raged on.

Poor Kurt had nowhere to go

I didn't want to leave him behind.
He had become my closest friend.

The road we had traveled together
Couldn't be understood by another.

There are times in life when everything
Seems to stretch ahead of us and time

Slows down, almost like a dream. We
Had been caught under the same spell.

I asked Kurt if he'd like to go back
To my town with me and Father Josef.

He was surprised, and sat in the corner
Of the shelter to think it over for a while.

Father Josef said to me, "Perhaps your
Parents won't want to feed and board him."

I said, "He can live and work on a farm."
Poor Kurt decided to come along.

My family was reunited

Mother and Father took turns
Holding on to me and
Standing back to look at me
To see how much I'd grown.

My grandparents pinched
My cheeks and shed tears.

Clara pulled me into
The house to see her new doll
And books. Schatze was
Probably the happiest to see me.
She licked my hands and face
And jumped on my back
When I bent down.

It was funny
To see my house
And family
Since I had
Gone out in the world.

I used to think it was all there was.

I had tucked my teddy bear

Into Paul's baby blanket
Before I left the cabin.

I always felt glad
About that later on.

The fairy tale book
I left with Nelly.

I wondered if she
Could still believe in
Happily ever after?

Poor Kurt's Surprise

My family looked at this strange person.
He would have to take a bath if he was
To come into the house and eat at the table.
I got in the large tub first and turned on
The faucet. Warm water tickled my body.

Usually more than one person shared the
Same water, but it was so dirty when I was
Finished, I unstopped the drain. And Mother
Filled it again. I was sitting at the kitchen
Table, eating a piece of apple strudel as

Poor Kurt washed then shaved. When
He came out of the bathroom I could
Hardly believe it! He was a young man,
Maybe eighteen years old,
With fine black hair and dreamy eyes.

Poor Kurt's Story

"The name my
People gave me is
Walthar Bihani.

I lived in Hadamar.
I saw the Disabled
Children arrive in buses.

Afterward the sky
Smelled of that
Terrible smoke.

I was afraid
They would come
For me too.

I wasn't Disabled.
I was part Gypsy,
Or Romani.

I was surprised
I could grow
A full beard.

I smeared it
With gray
Ashes.

I thought no one
Would ask questions
If I were an old beggar

I traveled alone
For weeks
Out of loneliness

And hunger.
When I arrived
At the shelter

They called me
Poor Kurt.

The Church
Had not expressed
Sympathy for
Persecuted Gypsies.

So I didn't reveal
My true identity
To Father Michael.

I lived in fear of
Being discovered.
Then I met Paula."

We looked at
Each other
And smiled.

Old Marthe was willing

To give Walthar a chance. She hired
Him to tend to her land and animals.
It turned out he had real skill in training
Horses. Once I saw him ride a mare
Standing on her back with his eyes
Closed and arms crossed. It must
Have been a kind of Gypsy magic.
He lived in the attic of Marthe's house.
If someone asked about him,
She threatened to punish them with
A hex. I enjoyed going to visit him.

I had romantic ideas about Walthar

He was three years
Older than I,
But that didn't matter.
I would grow up.

It was better
To be friends
Before husband
And wife.

His hair was like
The wing of a blackbird.
His long arms reached up
To the higher branches of a tree.

He could ride a bicycle
Backwards in the rain,
Singing, "I will steal
A little horse and our
Fortunes make thereby . . . "

My family seemed to approve

Walthar used Sign
With me
And soon my parents
And Clara and some
Of our neighbors
Understood too.

Father said
After the war
I could go to
A special school
In another town
For Deaf teenagers,
If it was still standing.

In truth,
It had to be rebuilt.
Germany's Deaf
Community
Never completely
Recovered

From the public
And personal
Destruction.

Father said
He was sorry
He hadn't thought
Of getting me
The best education
Before the war.

In 1943, the spring thawed

Our land, but our country was fighting
With the whole world, it seemed.
My experience had taught me

That Germany's cause was wrong. I was lucky
To have parents who were kind and taught
Us not to hate anybody. Could I make a
Difference, like Father Michael?

I thought of the future world—if Jews,
Gypsies, and the Disabled would have an
Equal part in it? Meanwhile, the sweet
Brook flowed and I slept on the hammock.

I was almost happy when summer's bees
And dandelions were replaced with a hard
Freeze and dark winter days. It had
Seemed wrong to feel so safe and alive.

Christmas Eve, 1943

The Christkind
Brought us a tree
And presents.

Walthar gave me
A boy and girl
He carved
Out of wood.

The next day
We had a roast
Goose lunch.

Outside
Snow fell
On my house

And other parts
Of Europe,
Lightly

Covering
The mass graves
Of the Nazis' victims,
And our fallen soldiers,

Young German
Boys who had
Given their lives
To an unjust cause.

I held on to Mother

As she and everybody else sang—
I had started to speak, but mostly
Croaked like a frog—
A song by our countrymen,
Father Josef Mohr and Franz Gruber.

Silent night, Holy night
All is calm, all is bright
'Round yon virgin Mother and Child
Holy infant so tender and mild.
Sleep in heavenly peace
Sleep in heavenly peace.

It was a prayer that year, not just a carol.
Our Savior's birth was tinged with sorrow.

I never saw

Stephanie Holderlin
Again.
But she was
In my heart.

Father Josef
Remained
A family friend.
Father Michael
Was killed
By an Allied bomb.

Later we learned
That six million
Jews
Had been
Murdered.

But I always
Thought
Of those seven
In the cabin.

The End

In May of 1945,
Germany
Surrendered.

The United States,
Russia, and England
Were victorious.

Japan and Italy
Fell with us.
Our crimes

Would live in
Infamy.
Forty-eight million

People had died
Fighting
Across the globe.

Grandmother said,
“All the suffering,
All the casualties.

This is the worst
War the world
Will ever know.”

I prayed to God, our
Lantern in the dark,
That it would be so.

In 1947

Father Josef married me and Walthar
In a country church ceremony. I wore
A long white gown and satin slippers.
I braided my hair and pinned it around
My head, like a crown. I proudly wore

A necklace of gold coins Walthar had
Given me when he proposed. It was
A Romani tradition. My groom had no
Family left after the war, so he decided
To join my world. Still, on our wedding

Night, we shared some salted bread before
Going to bed, another Gypsy custom. We
Had a son and daughter: one with dark,
Faraway eyes, the other with hair like spun
Gold. I was a farmer's wife. We visited

Father and Mother until they died, four
 months
Apart, in the same bed. Clara married too,
And became an actress in Berlin. Whatever
Season, whatever weather, we were glad we

Had survived the worst, but we also felt guilty.
That feeling—that we had escaped when
 others equally
Important had died—would never subside.

Postscript

A plaque
commemorating
The victims
of Action T4
Was set in
the pavement
Where the offices
once stood.
The original
building
Had been destroyed
in the war.
Educating
people is
The best tool
we have
Against
forgetting.
We must
make sure

Nothing

like T4

Ever

happens

Again.

And so

My story

told in

Poetry

ends.

Notes from the Author

Paula Becker is named after the German painter Paula Modersohn-Becker (1876–1907). The Nazis labeled her art, mainly portraits of peasant girls and women, "degenerate." She was a close friend of the great German poet Rainier Maria Rilke (1875–1926). Rilke's wife, the sculptor Clara Westhoff (1878–1954), was Paula's closest friend.

"Hear the Voice of the Poet" was inspired by the English poet William Blake's "Introduction," the first poem in his book Songs of Experience (1794).

Unfortunately, the practice of pouring hot wax into a person's ears to cure deafness was more common than it should have been into the twentieth century.

I thank Merriam Webster's online student dictionary for the neutral definition of euthanasia.

"The Story of Anny Wodl" is taken from an English translation of testimony given at the Nuremberg trials.
I borrowed Frederich Holderlin's last name for Stephanie. Holderlin (1770–1843) was a major German lyric poet.

Nelly and Paul, two of the children in the cabin, were named after Nelly Sachs (1891–1970) and Paul Celan (1920–1970)—the two greatest German Jewish poets of the Holocaust. Sachs was awarded the 1966 Nobel Prize in Literature; Celan committed suicide in Paris.

It is believed that 200,000 to 2,000,000 Gypsies were killed in the Romani Holocaust, also called Porajmos, which means "devouring" in the Romani language.

For readers, teachers, and parents interested in learning more about the Nazi's Action T4 euthanasia program, a good place to start is the online exhibition on the United States Holocaust Memorial Museum website, Deadly Medicine: Creating the Master Race. The book that originally got me interested in the subject is *Crying Hands: Eugenics and Deaf People in Nazi Germany,* by Horst Biesold (Gallaudet University Press).

Many thanks to my sister, Jean Marie LeZotte, my brother, Peter George LeZotte, and my sister-in-law, Jennifer LeZotte. And to my dog friend/helper May, her dog Basho, and Pebbles and Twister for keeping me laughing.

Special thanks to Sid Fleischman, Shelly Ruble, Mari Lu Grant, my Dog Wood Park friends, Jenny Moussa, and to my editor, Margaret Raymo, for seeing what I was trying to do and helping me do it—beyond what I'd ever imagined.

About the Author

Ann Clare LeZotte is completely deaf from a birth defect and illness. As a young girl in Long Island, New York, she banged her head for hours at a time and created her own world. She had a percentage of hearing in one ear during her grade school years, which helped her learn to speak, lip read, and assimilate into hearing culture. She has gone through years where she communicated mostly using a pad and pencil. She learned American Sign Language in her early twenties. A 1991 graduate of Sarah Lawrence College, she has had her poems published in the *American Poetry Review,* the *New Republic,* and the *Threepenny Review.* She received fellowships from Hedgebrook, the MacDowell Colony, VCCA, and Yaddo, as well as a Rona Jaffe Foundation Writers' Award. She lives in Gainesville, Florida, with her younger sister and their three dogs and one cat.